The Tractor Princess

Flora was the oiliest, muddiest princess who ever lived. She hated baths as much as the Queen hated spiders, and would tease poor Nanny by dancing on the furniture and singing "Clean me when you catch me". She was a pale thin child, for she would not eat the nice sensible food Nanny made for her, but after her visit to the transport café with Chaucer the chauffeur she had:

> pie and mash on Mondays
> spam and eggs on Tuesdays
> faggots and peas on Wednesdays
> sausage and beans on Thursdays
> fish and chips on Fridays
> curried eggs on Saturdays and
> corned beef stew on Sundays

and Flora was soon the strongest person in the palace.

Kathy Still

The Tractor Princess

Illustrated by John Bendall

Young Lions

First published in Great Britain by
Orchard Books 1989
First published in Young Lions 1990

Young Lions is an imprint of
the Children's Division, part of
Harper Collins Publishers Ltd,
8 Grafton Street, London W1X 3LA

Set in Baskerville
Printed and bound in Great Britain by
William Collins Sons & Co. Ltd, Glasgow

for Becky and her friends

CONTENTS

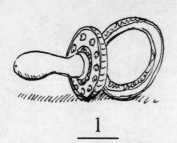

1

THE ROYAL BABY

Alone in the Atlantic Ocean, a little nearer Ireland than America, there is an island. Not many people know about it, for it lies just on the fold of the map and is rarely mentioned in the newspapers. Nevertheless, it is very green and pleasant, and has everything an island should, from icy mountains in the middle to sandy coves around the edge. Towards the north there lies a great city with an ancient cathedral and a splendid palace, which is the home of the King and Queen. They have nine musical sons, and were very happy indeed when their last child, a daughter, was born.

"She shall be dressed in only the finest silk

and lace," said the Queen, "and she shall have ringlets tied with satin ribbons."

"She shall have a little golden carriage drawn by two white ponies," said the King.

"And we shall sing lullabies and play sweet music to her," said her Nine Musical Brothers.

"And she shall have a pretty nursery, with bears and bunnies on every wall," said the Royal Nanny.

For many days they argued over what to

10

call the little girl. Finally it was agreed that
everybody could choose one name.

Her father liked Marigold, her mother pre-
ferred Belinda.

Her brothers chose Clara, Cecilia, Isolde,
Ophelia, Cosima, Constanze, Lucia, Susanna
and Carmen.

Nanny added Forget-me-not.

Then nobody could remember her name, so
they called her Flora for short.

But Princess Flora was a dreadful baby.

She screamed and cried and shook her fists. She was so angry that she couldn't drink her bottle, and then she would scream even more because she was so hungry.

No one knew what to do.

The doctor examined her and said "a touch of colic". Nanny rocked her, the Queen sang to her, the King pulled funny faces at her, the Nine Musical Brothers played lullabies for her, but she only cried more loudly than before.

Every day, Nanny dressed the little Princess in a pink and white coat and bonnet and wheeled her through the palace gardens in her pram. She showed her birds and butterflies and brought her flowers and leaves, but the Princess showed no interest at all. She simply glowered at everything around her.

"She is quite unlike her brothers," thought the Royal Nanny sadly.

The King and Queen were so delighted to have a baby daughter that she was often passed round on State Occasions. But the little Princess was not pleased. She blew raspberries at the Ladies-in-waiting. She stuck out her tongue at the British Ambassador. She did something dreadful on the Archbishop's knee and woke him up. And all the time she glared at everyone. She was quite the crossest baby in the kingdom.

"If only she would smile," said everyone in despair. "She is such a very unhappy child."

One day, when the little Princess was a few months old, there was a great commotion outside the palace. Workmen were arriving with drills and diggers, tractors and bull-dozers, cement-mixers and a huge crane.

"Strike a light," said the King in amazement. "It's the Gas Board."

He had sent for them the day after he was crowned, but that was so long ago he had quite forgotten why. He was still trying to remember when a lorry-load of pipes arrived.

"Of course! They've come to connect us!" he cried. "Now we shall have hot water."

The men set to work at once, hurrying to fetch water and boil kettles. When they had read their papers and drunk their tea, they began drilling and digging below the nursery window.

"I do hope the noise won't upset little Flora," said the Queen. "She is such a fretful child."

Upstairs in the nursery, the little Princess was unusually quiet. So quiet that Nanny became worried, and went over to the cot.

But Baby Flora was actually smiling.

"Wind," grunted Nanny (who was horribly practical) and she carried her to the window, patting her back.

As the little Princess looked out, a change came over her. She beamed and pointed and giggled and clapped her hands and laughed.

Nanny was astonished. She sent for the Nurserymaid, who ran to fetch the Queen,

who told the King, who called the Nine
Musical Brothers. But when they all arrived
at the door of the nursery, the workmen were
having a tea break. The only sound was that
of the little Princess crying — not her usual
angry yell, but a terribly sad, disappointed
sort of noise.

Then a voice outside shouted "O.K. lads" and work began again. Men drilled and diggers dug, the crane swung high over the roof-tops, and a tractor collided with a bulldozer.

Everyone in the nursery put their hands to their ears, for the noise was unbearable. Then they looked at Flora. As she looked out of the window, a huge smile spread across her face, and once again she began to giggle and gurgle and point and clap her hands. The Royal Family was delighted.

The King hugged the Queen, the Nine Musical Brothers danced and twirled about the room, the Nurserymaid sang a hymn, and Nanny was left holding the baby.

The King dreaded little Flora being upset again when the noise stopped. So he went downstairs and asked the workmen if they would very much mind taking their tea in turns.

They thought for a moment, then shook their heads and said "Not possible".

"Something has to be done," said the King, and went to see the foreman.

At lunchtime the King did not appear. The Queen shut the dining-room window, for the noise of the drills was dreadful. But when she looked out, all the gas men were having a tea break.

Then she saw the King and the Head Footman, juddering wildly about below Flora's window. The King was having a wonderful time using his drill as a pogo stick, but the Head Footman seemed very hot and cross. His drill jumped around so much that now and again his wig fell off and then all the workmen clapped and shouted "Encore".

All afternoon the little Princess gurgled contentedly in her cot, while the King fidgeted and tapped his crown, waiting his next turn with the drill. And all night, while the palace slept, the King and Queen sat up in bed wondering how they could make their baby daughter happy. At sunrise the King summoned the palace painters and decorators, and the Queen sent for Nanny.

That morning the little Princess did not wear her pink coat and bonnet. Nor did she sit glaring at the gardens from her pram. Instead, Nanny wheeled her through the city streets, and all the people waved and cheered as Flora passed by in a shiny yellow helmet and donkey jacket. She sat up very straight and waved and smiled and everyone said she looked just like her mother. (She didn't, of

course.) Nanny parked the pram at the edge of a huge building site and settled down to knit pink fluffy things for proper babies.

Flora had never been so contented. So Nanny knitted herself some grey woollen earplugs and took her to visit a different building site or roadworks every day. Whether it was a factory chimney coming down or a multi-storey going up, baby Flora was sure to be there. On Sunday mornings the chauffeur took her to a busy garage on the motorway to see the car-wash.

Meanwhile, the Nine Musical Brothers were very busy. They made a tape recording of all the noisiest machines in the kingdom, as well as pipes gurgling, bus conductors singing, and aeroplanes coming in to land.

The nursery was completely repainted. There was no trace of the bears and bunnies that had once danced round its walls. Now there were trucks and tractors, diggers and dustcarts; four fire-engines, a car transporter, and a huge golden crane with the royal coat-of-arms on the cab. When she saw it, Flora cooed softly and blew bubbles.

Nanny bit her lip and counted to a hundred.

Within the first five minutes of listening to the Nine Musical Brothers' tape baby Flora had fallen into a deep and peaceful sleep. The yellow bunny which hung at the side of the cot and played tinkly lullabies had always disturbed Flora, so it was given to the gardener's daughter.

A few days later, Nanny sent the Nursery-maid to fetch the King and Queen again.

"The dear Princess has spoken her first word," she told them.

With tears in her eyes the Queen stepped over to the cot and peered at her only daughter.

"Say Mu-mmy," she cooed. "Mum - mum - mum - mum - mum."

But the little Princess glared up at her and said, "TRACTOR."

And ever since that day, the Princess Marigold Belinda Clara Cecilia Isolde Ophelia Cosima Constanze Lucia Susanna Carmen Forget-me-not has been known as the Tractor Princess.

2

THE LITTLE PRINCESS

Little Flora was so unlike the rest of her family that her mother often wondered whether she had been given the right baby when she left hospital.

Flora's brothers were pink and shiny and had nice manners. Every morning they folded their pyjamas neatly, and on Saturdays they tidied their bedrooms and dusted their fossils. But Flora was quite different.

The Queen loved fine clothes and long mirrors to see them in. She wept at weddings and kissed babies wherever she went. But Flora was quite different.

The King always obeyed the Queen. But Flora didn't.

Flora was the oiliest, muddiest princess who ever lived. She hated baths as much as the Queen hated spiders, and would tease poor Nanny by dancing on the furniture and singing "Clean me when you catch me".

But washing Flora was much easier than dressing her.

"Little princesses must wear pretty dresses," Nanny said every morning. And every morning Flora kicked and screamed and shouted until she gave up and let her stay in her pyjamas.

One day the Royal Dressmaker came into the nursery carrying a suitcase.

"No more pretty dresses," shouted Flora. "When I am Queen I shall have you beheaded."

But she had a surprise when she looked inside the suitcase. Instead of frilly frocks and lacy tights there were T-shirts and trousers, tracksuits and trainers; and everything had a little orange tractor sewn onto it. Flora hugged the dressmaker and put all her new clothes on at once.

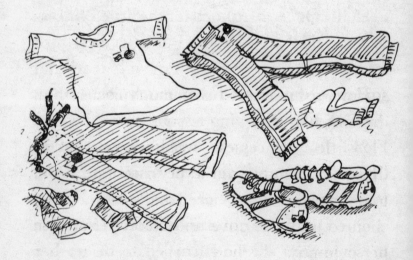

Every month Flora's Nine Musical Brothers held a concert at the palace to which everyone was invited.

The Queen thought it would be very nice if Flora could take part, so she arranged for her to have singing lessons. But after her first lesson the singing master left with a terrible headache and was never seen again.

So the Queen arranged for the Tractor Princess to have piano lessons. But after her second lesson the piano teacher sent a postcard to say he was living in Australia.

So the Queen arranged for the little Princess to have dancing lessons. But after her third lesson the dancing master burst into tears and said he was going to become a typist.

"Can I have driving lessons now?" begged Flora. But the Queen wouldn't hear of it. "Flora's talent has yet to be discovered," she told people.

The Queen had promised Flora a surprise present when she had learned to tie up her shoe-laces. But the surprise turned out to be a doll's pram. Flora put all her dolls inside and pushed it into the lake.

"All I want is a tractor," she wailed.

And someone must have heard because a week later a big shiny toy tractor was standing in the palace yard. It was blue with lots of stickers and came with a very useful trailer. Flora stared at it in amazement. "Oi!" she shouted to a King and Queen who had come to see her parents. "I've got wheels."

She pedalled round to show Nanny, who was doing her exercises in the rose garden.

But Nanny said, "What a horrid thing! You must give it to a poor child who has no toys."

"Not likely," thought Flora, and began to chase her. Over the hill and round the lake ... through the woods and up to the Temple, where at last poor Nanny leapt onto a stone lion to get out of her way. And as she leapt, her handbag fell open and hatpins and peppermints flew everywhere. Flora kindly stopped to pick them up, then pedalled back to the palace to show Chaucer her wonderful present.

Chaucer was the King's chauffeur, and Flora's very best friend. It was widely known that if it hadn't been for him, the little Princess might have wasted away to nothing.

She was a pale thin child, for she would not eat the nice sensible food Nanny made for her.

She spat out her greens and dribbled her broth; she oozed her prunes and refused her rusks. And all the time she grew paler and thinner. Her brothers brought her quails' eggs and little pieces of wild boar from the dining room, but she wouldn't eat those either. No one knew what to do.

One day, the King and Queen went to the harbour to choose a new yacht. On the way back it grew foggy. Chaucer stopped the car at a transport café.

"We can go no further until the fog has cleared," he said.

Inside the café the Queen wrinkled her nose

and nibbled a cup cake, while the King played pinball with a couple of truckdrivers. Chaucer sat at the counter, eating some supper. The little Princess stood beside him, looking so pale and thin he felt sorry for her.

He gave her a few chips. And she ate them.

He gave her a sausage. And she ate that.

Then he gave her a piece of fried bread and she ate that too.

The Queen looked on in amazement.

"I would like some of that for my daughter," she told the enormous lady behind the counter.

"All day breakfast for the Princess," shouted the lady to a hole in the wall.

"All day breakfast coming up," replied the hole.

By the time the fog had cleared, Flora had

eaten three helpings of everything. The Queen asked for a menu to take home to Nanny. From then on Flora had:

pie and mash on Mondays
spam and eggs on Tuesdays
faggots and peas on Wednesdays
sausage and beans on Thursdays
fish and chips on Fridays
curried eggs on Saturdays
and corned beef stew on Sundays.

And every day Nanny would shake her head and say: "This is no way to bring up a child!" as she brought Flora's dish to the table. But she had to admit that she was growing bigger and stronger all the same.

Flora was soon the strongest person in the palace, and ready to help wherever she was needed. She undid bottles for the butler and jam-jars for the cook; she cracked the nuts at Christmas and opened windows that had been stuck for centuries.

She was not only strong but brave too. She rescued the King's kite and the cook's cat from trees; she fixed an aerial to the tallest turret; and one night she chased off a newsman with the Queen's trident. "Whatever should we do without her?" people asked one another.

The King and Queen were very grateful to Chaucer, but they did wish Flora wouldn't spend so much time with him. Every day she would sit on an oily rag at the back of the garage and watch him as he worked. Sometimes he brought over little bits of engine to show her, which she would study carefully before cleaning on her clothes.

As she grew bigger, Chaucer taught her everything he knew about cars and engines, as well as a lot of rather naughty things to say when they went wrong. And when there was time to spare, he would make her laugh with

all the clever tricks he had learned as a boy in the circus.

He and Flora were greatly looking forward to the Queen's birthday when a concert was to be held in her honour. All kinds of important people had been invited and just for once, as it was a special occasion, Nanny agreed to let Flora stay up, too.

At eight o'clock the curtain rose and the Nine Musical Brothers began to sing. The Queen put on her listening-to-music-face and hummed along; the King chuckled at his joke book; the Lords and Ladies listened and clapped politely, and were all ready to leap from their seats in the interval when the Queen's eldest son, Prince Igor, came back onto the stage. There was a lot of excited whispering in the audience: he was surely going to announce his engagement. But he didn't. Instead he said:

"Ladies and Gentlemen — the Tractor Princess."

Up in the Royal Box, the King poked the Queen in the ribs.

"Do you know anything about this?" he asked.

"Certainly not," snapped the Queen, as Flora rode her tractor onto the stage. She was followed by Chaucer, who wore a glittery costume that looked rather tight for him. They both bowed; then he handed her some things from the trailer, and the show began.

First, she played some folk songs on the spoons. Then she lifted some very heavy weights. And finally she juggled with the crown jewels, and didn't drop a single ring.

The audience whistled and cheered and stamped their feet; ladies threw their lapdogs in the air, and a footman fainted. Everyone shouted "More! More!", but it was time for

the Nine Musical Brothers to sing their song about spring.

Nobody wanted to leave at the end of the concert. The people clapped slowly, chanting, "We want Flora! We want Flora!" until Nanny came onto the stage. She waved her finger sternly at the Lords and Ladies. "The Princess is fast asleep in bed," she told them. "And it's high time you were, too, for I'm sure you all have ships to launch in the morning."

There is no point in arguing with Nanny, so everyone left and a footman turned out the lights.

High up, and all alone, sat the Queen in the Royal Box. She took out a handkerchief and thought sadly to herself: "How happy I would be if she could dance ... but she did curtsey nicely."

That wasn't quite the end of the story. The Queen was so pleased with Chaucer that she gave him a gadget for cleaning the car, and appointed him Master of the Rolls in her Birthday Honours List.

3

THE DUSTMEN

Early one morning Flora woke up feeling very happy. It was Nanny's day off and Chaucer had promised to let her change the oil in the Landrover. As Nanny left she said to Flora, "If you are careful you may play with my button box whilst I am out."

The moment she had gone, the Tractor Princess said something very rude about Nanny's button box, and ran as fast as she could to the garage. But when she arrived there was no sign of Chaucer or the car.

"He's taken the Queen to open a telephone exchange," said the man who fed the peacocks. "Her Majesty saw a mouse in the helicopter."

Flora was disappointed. There had been no rain for a week and all the puddles had dried up; her Nine Musical Brothers were on a Royal Tour; and the King was having his portrait painted for a new set of stamps.

There was nothing to do and no one for her to play with.

She wandered into the kitchen and ate some of the cat's food.

All of a sudden there came a mighty rumbling and churning, and a dustcart bumped into the palace yard. Flora went outside to take a look. She walked all round with her hands in her pockets, then climbed into the cab beside the driver.

"Your exhaust pipe's loose," she said. "And one of your rear wheel nuts is missing."

The man put down his newspaper, and was very surprised to see a real Princess.

"Thank you for telling me, Your Highness," he said. "I'll get that fixed at the depot."

"It's nice up here," said Flora, looking all

round. "May I come for a ride?"

But before the driver could reply, another dustman tapped her on the arm. "We'd like to introduce ourselves," he said.

So Flora jumped down from the cab and shook hands with Sidney, Scott, Horace and Arnold (who were twins) and Olaf, a jolly Norwegian dustman on an exchange visit. The driver was called Milton. He leaned out of the cab and smiled at Flora.

"Go and ask your Dad if you can come. But hurry!"

Flora bounded indoors and ran up the stairs and along the line of marble gentlemen, past the pictures of pale pink ladies, and into the Throne Room to see the King. He sat very still while he was being painted, and didn't turn his head when she came in.

"May I help the dustmen today?" she begged.

"I don't see why not," said the King in a funny voice, trying not to move his lips. "Just make sure Nanny doesn't hear about it."

Flora blew him a kiss and was back in the palace yard in no time.

"I can come," she shouted, and the dustmen cheered. She climbed into the cab and off they went.

The dustcart was bigger and noiser than all the King's cars put together. As they went along the dustmen sang "Clementine" and "Waltzing Matilda"and Flora joined in. They stopped in a street of tall thin houses and lined up on the pavement.

"Where do I start?" asked Flora.

The dustmen were shocked. They all began to talk at once.

"But you're a princess" "You'll get dirty" "You're too little" "You couldn't possibly carry a dustbin" "Luvaduck" they said.

While they were all carrying on, Flora fetched a dustbin and stood it by the dustcart.

"Will one of you empty that for me?" she asked. "I can't quite reach."

The Tractor Princess was a great help that morning. She fetched a lot of bins and Horace emptied them; but she didn't carry them back again. Instead she tipped them on their sides then leapt up and trundled them along, just as

Chaucer had shown her. People stood at their front gates and marvelled at her skill. Nobody recognised her because she was so dirty, and by the time the dustcart had reached the end of the road, quite a crowd had gathered. A hot cross policeman pushed his way through to find out what was happening.

"What's this kid doing with you?" he shouted. "She should be at home with her mother, not messing around with dustbins."

Flora jumped down from her bin and stood up very straight.

"I am on a Royal Walkabout," she said haughtily. "And my mother is busy opening a telephone exchange."

All the people cheered and the policeman grew quite scarlet. He bowed and apologised and bowed again. Then he said, "Er — I think I can see a burglar," and ran off as fast as he could.

The last street on the dustmen's round was long and wide and lined with plane trees. People outside the pavement cafés waved and smiled as Flora bowled past on an empty bin. She was joined by an Italian waiter, who ran beside her playing his violin; then an ice cream man caught up with them and gave Flora a huge cornet topped with nuts and cherries. Halfway along the street a flower-seller showered them all in white carnations, and the dustmen picked them up and put them in their buttonholes.

There was a great gathering of Nannies and babies outside a café called *Sensible Snax*. The babies laughed and pointed and bounced up and down in their prams when they saw Flora. She stuck out her tongue at them, which made them giggle and dribble all down their little woollen coats. The Nannies stopped eating their rice pudding and said "Tut-tut! Whatever next?"

"Such silly antics," said one.

"Too much television," said another.

"I blame the parents," said a third.

"Whatever's going on?" asked a cross voice. "I haven't got my glasses."

Flora nearly fell off her dustbin. So this was where Nanny went on her day off! She darted down a side alley, ran round the block, and hid in a telephone box until the dustmen reached the end of the street.

"What's the matter?" asked Sidney. "You look as if you've seen a ghost."

"Ghosts don't eat rice pudding," said Flora weakly, and sat down with a bump.

At lunchtime Horace went to a baker's shop and came back with sausage rolls, meat pies in little shiny dishes, sugar doughnuts and plastic cups of bright orange soup. Then they

drove to a nice sunny roundabout to eat it all. Milton said grace; then each dustman took a white linen napkin from his pocket and tucked it under his chin. They ate in silence, and when they had finished they dabbed their mouths and threw their cups and dishes into the back of the dustcart. Then they sat in the

sun and talked. Olaf took a bundle of photographs from his pocket and handed them round. There were pictures of his workmates at home; his boss; his goldfish; himself as a baby, and then as a troll at a Christmas party, and finally a picture of his parents.

"Why haven't your mummy and daddy got their crowns on?" asked Flora, and all the dustmen laughed and slapped their knees and said "Luvaduck". Then the cathedral clock struck two. They all groaned and climbed back into the cab.

"Are we going to collect more rubbish?" asked Flora hopefully.

"Not now," said Arnold. "We're off to the tip."

When they reached the edge of the city, Milton turned off the main road and into a very odd avenue. Instead of trees it was lined with all kinds of old and broken things that nobody wanted. Flora saw wardrobes and armchairs, sideboards and bedsteads; televisions, washbasins, birdcages, clocks, sinks, baths, beds, cars, vans, bikes, prams, and even a stuffed camel with a leg missing. At the end of the track the rubbish was piled high, and leaned over to make a wobbly arch, just held together by brambles and creeper. And on the other side of the arch lay the tip.

It was the biggest hole Flora had ever seen.

"Oh, do let me dump the rubbish, please," she begged, as Milton backed up to the edge of the hole.

"But it's Horace's turn," said Arnold.

"It's all right," said Horace bravely. "I don't mind really."

So Flora pressed the big red button on the dashboard, and WHOOSH! everything tumbled out of the dustcart and into the tip.

"Are you thirsty?" asked Sidney, and Flora nodded. So they all walked over to a little tin hut, which looked very drab and dirty from the outside, but inside it was all fresh flowers and

rosy wallpaper. There were six round tables with crisp white cloths, and a dresser stacked with best bone china. Sidney rang a little brass bell, and an enormous lady looked out from a hatch. When she saw Milton she ran over and hugged him.

"This is Shelley," he told Flora, who smiled and held out her hand. Shelley recognised the Tractor Princess at once. She shrieked "Lawks-a-mercy! Who'd have thought ...?" and hugged her too.

The dustmen sat down at one of the little tables.

"What'll it be today, boys?" asked Shelley. "Earl Grey, China or Darjeeling?"

Milton ordered Earl Grey tea and saffron cakes all round. While they were waiting Flora stood at the doorway and gazed out over the tip. She watched a great white crane as it scooped up huge jawfuls of rubbish, swung them across the sky, and dropped them into a barge on the canal. When the barge was piled

52

high it slowly chugged off, and another moved forward to take its place. Then it began to rain; and a moment later the sun came out, and with the sun came a glorious rainbow. The Tractor Princess clasped her hands and sniffed the air.

"If I could look out of my window and see this every day I would never be bored," she told the dustmen. "But all I can see is a rotten old temple, and that's ruined."

After tea they sat dangling their legs over the edge of the tip and played Rubbish I-Spy until the day's work was done. Then they drove back to the palace, and this time Milton went through the grand entrance and parked by a statue of Flora's Granny. A footman ran

to tell the King and Queen that the Princess and her friends were downstairs.

"I think we should ask them in," said the Queen.

So the King went to ask the dustmen if they would like a glass of sherry. They all agreed that was a nice idea, and followed him to the Throne Room. One by one the dustmen bowed as Flora introduced them to the Queen. She smiled and waved them towards a pair of gold scrolly sofas with red cushions. They all sat down and the butler brought round a tray of sherry. The Queen sipped hers and said, "Now I want you to tell me all about rubbish."

When Nanny returned home that evening she expected to find Flora fast asleep in her nursery, but there was no sign of her. She went downstairs to look for her and noticed a funny smell — surely it was coming from the throne room? Hearing voices, she peeped in, and was shocked at what she saw.

The Queen was slapping her knees and laughing, while the King cried with mirth, and the filthiest Flora she had ever seen sat with a row of even dirtier men. They were sitting on the Queen's nice sofas and drinking sherry out of the best cut glasses.

"This isn't really happening," Nanny told herself. "I need a milky drink and an early night."

"Do join us, Nanny," called the Queen, seeing her in the doorway. "Olaf has been telling us all about things he's found in Norwegian dustbins."

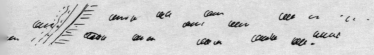

Nanny sat down as far away from the smelly dustmen as possible, and decided to look for another job in the morning; Flora sighed happily and hugged her knees, and Olaf brought out his photographs again. The King laughed so much at the picture of his goldfish that he began to hiccup; he laughed and hiccuped all the more when the dustmen dropped cold keys down his back. Nanny had seen enough. She marched poor Flora straight to the bathroom, and no one, not even the Queen, dared argue.

A week later an envelope arrived for the dustmen.

"Whatever can it be?" they asked one another, for it had a red wax seal and was as long as three dustbins.

Inside was a sticker to put on the wind-screen of their dustcart. In big white letters it said: BY APPOINTMENT TO H.R.H. THE TRACTOR PRINCESS and the Royal coat-of-arms was printed at either end.

And when he saw that, even the depot manager called them "Sir".

4

THE ROYAL WEDDING

After breakfast one morning the Queen sent for the whole family.

"This is a very happy day for us all," she said, and burst into tears. So the King went on to tell everyone that the Queen's younger brother, Prince Hugo, was to marry his friend Gloriana. Flora was unimpressed.

"Is that all?" she asked.

The King smiled at her. "It will be a very special day for you, too, Flora. They want you to be a bridesmaid."

The Tractor Princess was beside herself. She jumped up and down and screamed and shouted all the naughty words she had learned from Chaucer.

"If you use any of those words ever again, you'll have dancing lessons," said the Queen angrily. "Now go and clean off that tractor oil, because you are to be measured for your dress this morning."

Preparations for the wedding were soon under way, and everyone except Flora was very excited. Her Nine Musical Brothers wrote something called an anthem, which they practised every morning. They cried as they played, for the tune was very sad and solemn. Gloriana got in everyone's way, and Hugo mooned about in the rose garden; the Queen spent lots of money, and all the while the King polished his crown nervously and wondered if they could afford it.

Presents for Hugo and Gloriana began to arrive by every post.

They soon had everything they might need for when they were married, from cut-glass lightbulbs to a set of invisible teaspoons. In

one parcel was an armadillo, which the Queen insisted on sending to the zoo until Hugo and his wife had found somewhere to live. Foreign Kings and Queens sent old dark paintings and chiming clocks; and from all over the kingdom came the breakfast things. There were kettles and coffee-pots, egg-timers and egg-poachers, things for taking the tops off boiled eggs, and a toaster for every day of the year.

"What *do* married people do with toasters?" asked Flora, but no one answered.

The morning of the wedding was the worst poor Flora had ever known. First the Royal Dressmaker arrived, and began unpacking a large box. Flora gasped in horror at her dress. It had frills and ribbons and lace and bows and stuck right out. The dressmaker giggled.

"Don't worry, Your Highness, that's only the petticoat. Your dress is much prettier."

Then the Royal Hairdresser arrived. He pulled and twisted Flora's hair into a mass of golden ringlets, and used so much hairspray that they crunched like brandysnaps.

Then the Royal Shoemaker arrived. He gave Flora a pair of dainty golden slippers and a little gold bag to match. "Just big enough for your handkerchief," he said.

"What handkerchief?" snorted Flora.

Finally, the florist arrived with a ring of white flowers to pin in Flora's hair, and a posy tied with a lacy frill.

Nanny zipped and buttoned and hooked and tied the pretty dress onto Flora. She would have looked very beautiful if she hadn't scowled so.

"When you grow up you will marry a prince yourself," said Nanny.

"No I won't," said Flora. "I'll be a tractor driver."

When Nanny had finished, she busied herself with the other bridesmaids, who were called Camilla, Vanilla, Viola and Lettice. Flora looked about her. Everywhere people

were powdering noses, dabbing on scent, twisting and looking in mirrors, finding pins in their dresses and squealing. It really was awful.

Flora wandered into the courtyard to look at Gloriana's carriage, which was white and gold with cherubs on the roof and detectives inside. After that she waved to the guests as they set off for the cathedral, and when the last Lord had left, she took her place in the bridesmaids' coach. Poor Flora! She felt very sad and forlorn, for the other girls were terribly old and took no notice of her. They carried on about diets and dandruff, pimples and princes until the bride appeared, and then they all cried: "Isn't she beautiful?" Then they sighed: "What a simply heavenly dress." Flora thought, "She looks even sillier than I do," and felt much better. She put on her fiercest face and thought about tractors.

As they rode through the city streets with all the people clapping and cheering, Flora suddenly spotted her friends the palace dustmen. They were all standing rather dangerously on the roof of their dustcart waving a banner which read

WE ♥ THE TRACTOR PRINCESS

and cheering more loudly than anyone else. Flora stood up and waved and waved and quite forgot about being cross.

Soon they arrived at the cathedral. A shiny man in a top hat told Flora to take her place behind Lettice and Camilla.

"Just do as they do and you can't go wrong," he said.

Flora was so frightened of all the strange, staring faces that she did exactly as she had been told. She followed the other bridesmaids down the aisle and watched very carefully as they stood before the altar. When Camilla coughed, Flora coughed louder; and when Lettice scratched, she scratched even harder. The Queen wept and saw nothing, but she was very proud of her little daughter all the same.

Then the service began. There were hymns and prayers, followed by a lot of fuss about a ring, and then the Archbishop stood up and told all the people about a lady called Pauline Doctrine who was very obedient. When he had finished, the Nine Musical Brothers sang their anthem and Flora followed the bridesmaids into a little room so full of photographers she could hardly breathe.

"What's happening?" she asked in a small voice.

"They're signing the register," hissed Vanilla.

"It's a special book you write your name in when you get married," said Lettice in a dreamy voice. Then she looked at Flora. "You really ought not to blow bubbles," she said. "It'll ruin the photographs."

Then everyone began to leave the little room, and Flora followed, back through the staring faces, and into the open air.

Flora had never been so pleased to see Nanny, who was waiting for her outside the cathedral. She handed her a little box.

"This is confetti," she told Flora. "You must throw it at the bride."

Flora couldn't believe her ears. She looked first at the box and then at Nanny, who gave her a silly smile and pushed her forward.

"All this excitement's gone to her head," thought Flora as she rushed at Gloriana and hurled the box as hard as she could. It whizzed past her, and she ducked and squealed crossly. An elderly duke picked up the box and handed it back to the Tractor Princess.

"It's not usual to throw the whole packet, my dear," he said nicely. "Just the little bits of paper inside." And with that he took a handful of confetti and sprinkled it all over the Archbishop. Flora giggled. Weddings weren't so bad after all.

An annoying man was taking lots of photographs.

"Will the bridesmaids step forward, please?" he asked. "Thank you, dearies. Now, smile."

They all smiled for the camera. The Tractor Princess wore a wide and wonderful grin and thought, "Nobody's noticed! Not one of them!"

"I wonder who'll catch the bouquet?" Nanny said, with another soppy smile.

"Why should anyone catch it?" asked Flora.

"The bride always tosses her bouquet as she leaves the church, and the lucky girl who catches it will be the next to marry," replied Nanny.

Flora pulled a face. "I'd rather catch measles," she said.

And when Gloriana flung her bouquet into the crowd, Flora yelled "DUCK!" and leapt into a waiting carriage before Nanny could catch her. On the way back through the City all the people waved and cheered more loudly than ever, and the dustmen raised their glasses and sang "For She's a Jolly Good Fellow" as Flora went by.

The reception was a disappointment. There were plates of dainty cheesy things and fishy things, spicy meats and bowls of salad. There were pies and flans and roasted peacocks, creamy dips and things on sticks. Amid it all there stood a great white wedding cake, so high that a hole had been cut in the ceiling to make way for it. The last three layers were in the nursery, and the King led everyone upstairs to see the marzipan Royal Family which spun round and round on the top.

For a moment, Flora was alone: she saw her chance to escape and then spotted Chaucer, who was beckoning to her from a doorway.

"You have these," he said, handing her a packet. "I'll have something to eat in the kitchen.

Inside there were corned beef sandwiches, which were Flora's favourite, and some pickled onions. She fetched a plate and settled down in a corner to eat them.

The Queen spotted her daughter and called her over.

"Flora, I want you to meet Crown Prince Oswald," she said.

The Prince smiled very nicely and bowed. Then he said: "I say, are those corned beef sandwiches? I must have missed them," and hurried off towards the tables. Word soon got around, and everyone began to look for the corned beef sandwiches. In the end, the butler telephoned the nearest sandwich bar and ordered a hundred rounds, which disappeared in no time. The roasted peacocks were barely touched, and after everyone had left, Chaucer took one home for his mother, who was delighted.

That evening a grand ball was held at the palace. Outside in the courtyard, Flora jumped into a muddy puddle she had been saving all day. She took a matchbox from the little gold bag the Royal Shoemaker had given her, and let her woodlice out for a run.

"You have been a dear, sweet girl today," said the Queen when she came to kiss Flora goodnight. "I am so proud of you."

The next morning, the Queen could hardly wait to see the wedding photographs. She rang for some coffee and iced fancies, and settled into the cushions on the sofa. Her eyes filled with tears as she opened the album and it played the Musical Brothers' Anthem. She dabbed her eyes so that she could see the pictures better. Here were the bride and groom ... his family ... her family ... the groom with the best man ... the bride with her

71

father ... at last! Here were the bridesmaids, and there in the front row was dear little Flora, smiling and looking so beautiful in her dress.

Then the Queen looked very hard at the photograph. Quickly she turned the page and looked at another. But her eyes had not deceived her. That wicked child! In all the rush to get ready for the wedding, no one had

The ~AL WEDDING

noticed that Flora was not wearing her dainty golden slippers, but her dirty smelly trainers instead.

Poor Flora! The Queen found her a horrid old dancing master with a bad temper and a stick, and she had a lesson every day for a month.

The ~ROYAL WEDDING~

5

THE GARDEN PARTY

One afternoon Flora discovered a strange prince in the boot room. He was about the same age as herself, and wore a dented crown and an eggy shirt. Flora thought he looked rather nice, so she sat next to him and began an argument.

"My palace is bigger than your palace."

"Our kingdom's bigger than your kingdom."

"My great-great-great-great-granny was Mildred the Unwashed."

"That's nothing. Mine was a Vampire."

"We've got a new helicopter," boasted Flora.

"So what?" sneered the boy. "I've been sick on Concorde."

Flora was very impressed and wanted to hear all about it.

"What's your name?" she asked when the boy had finished. "Mine's Flora."

"I know," said the boy. "I'm cousin Hilary, and I've come for the garden party."

Flora was quite overcome. She took him straight down to the garage to meet Chaucer, and then up to the nursery for tea.

That night, Flora lay awake listening while Hilary told her all about his eleven enormous sisters who ran the Navy and tricycled for charity; and his palace, which was extremely

haunted and often struck by lightning. His parents were much too frightened to live there, so they stayed in a bungalow next door, along with a magician and an executioner.

"You children will have to amuse your-selves today," said Nanny at breakfast. "I shall be cleaning the cannons for the garden party."

Flora and Hilary tried very hard to look disappointed.

"Oh, I expect we'll find something to do," said the Tractor Princess. "Don't worry."

"Do you know how to play 'Havoc'?" asked Hilary when Nanny had left.

"No," said Flora curiously. "Never heard of it."

"I'll teach you," said Hilary. "The best place to begin is always in the kitchen."

That evening the King and Queen were watching the Jester when there came a knock at the door. In marched Nanny; followed by Cook; three Kitchen-maids; the Ironing Lady,

Viscount Lino and the Royal Panel-beater (who was also the man from the Union).

"Your Majesties," he said with a bow. "Either you do something about those children, or we go on strike at midnight."

"But you can't," said the Queen in alarm. "We've a garden party on Thursday."

"Exactly," said the man from the Union.

"What have they done?" asked the King.

It was Nanny who answered. She was quite pink with rage.

"They flushed a tapestry down the lavatory blocked the pipes and fused the lights and raced their ferrets across the terrace and tied a Peer to a chandelier . . ."

She paused for breath and then carried on:

"... they stopped the clocks with Hilary's socks and fired the guns and beat the drums and hurled a jelly and broke my telly and fell in the lake and ... well, that was it, really."

"Oh no it wasn't!" shouted Cook angrily. "They put petrol in my pastry. And I've no time to make any more before Thursday, so there'll be no jam tarts. Not one!"

"And they had a tug-of-war with my table-cloths," wept the Ironing Lady. "And I can't possibly do them all again, not with the foot-men's frilly shirts as well."

"Oh dear, oh dear, oh dear!" said the Queen. "Whatever shall we do?"

"Make the punishment fit the crime," said Nanny grimly.

So they did.

When Flora awoke the next morning, she was not in her cosy nursery, but in a cold, round room at the top of the East Tower. She padded across the cold stone floor and opened the door … but her way was barred by two stout guards.

"I'm awfully sorry, Your Highness," said one. "But we've been ordered to keep you under House Arrest until you've ironed all the tablecloths for the garden party."

And when Hilary awoke the next morning, he was not in the cosy nursery either, but in a cold round room at the top of the West Tower. A guard came in, carrying a tray, and on it was the biggest breakfast the little Prince had ever seen.

"You're going to need this," he said. "You've got work to do."

"What sort of work?" asked Hilary nervously.

"Making pastry," replied the guard with a grin. "Lots and lots of it."

For three days and three nights, the children were imprisoned in the towers, and everything ran very smoothly without them. Flora ironed and ironed until her arms ached, and she was too tired even to think of escaping. Cook was most impressed by Hilary's pastry, and sent him a plate of jam

tarts; but he paled at the sight of them and gave them to the guards.

On the morning of the garden party, the children were released, but on one condition.

"If you dare so much as to swap the flags on the sandwiches," the King told them sternly, "you will do all the washing up afterwards. Do I make myself clear?"

The children nodded miserably, and spent the morning in Nanny's room doing jigsaw puzzles, which worried her greatly.

At exactly three o'clock that afternoon, the footmen opened the gates, the Nine Musical Brothers struck up "Tea for Two", and the party began. The Tractor Princess and Hilary sat on the wall and watched the guests arrive. Many ladies had gone to great trouble to find suitable hats: the Bishop's wife was wearing

one with a rim and a veil and a hive of honey-bees on top, while the Admiral's mother was weighed down by a helicopter gunship.

"Cor!" said Flora. "I could do with a hat like that. Let's go and take a look."

But the children never did meet the Admiral's mother, for they were soon waylaid by other guests. There was the man who had climbed Everest carrying a spin-dryer, and another who had rolled all the way down the Matterhorn in a paper bag; a lady who had sailed the high seas on her dressing-table, and three dear old men who had floated round Australia on their backs.

Then there were the dreadfully bossy people who were on all sorts of committees; in no time at all they were organizing everyone else, so the King and Queen were able to sit down and have a nice quiet cup of tea.

"I can't abide them," said the Queen, "but every year I wonder what on earth we'd do if we didn't invite them."

She watched thankfully as they organized queues for the lavatories, plates for the sandwiches, sticks for the sausages and brooms for the breakages. They found a deckchair for a drunken Duke, and when everything was running smoothly, they started up a hearty game in which everyone had to burst a balloon.

"This is bad news," said Flora. So Hilary fetched a plate of sausages, and they crept behind a marquee to eat them. But to their surprise, they were not the only children there. . . .

Five little girls were skipping in a ring,

while five little boys were singing and making
daisy-chains. They were all dressed exactly
alike, with crisp white ruffles and tumbling
curls. When they saw Flora and Hilary, they
all bowed and curtseyed like clockwork.

"What on earth are you lot supposed to
be?" asked Flora rudely.

"We're the Best Behaved Children in the
Kingdom, Your Highness," they said
proudly.

"Who says?" demanded Hilary.

"We were chosen by *Hearth and Home* maga-
zine," said a tall girl, "out of thousands."

"So what are you doing in my garden?"
asked Flora crossly.

"Her Majesty the Queen was kind enough
to invite us," said the girl. "Would you like to
hear our song?"

"No fear!" yelled Flora and Hilary together, but the children lined up and began to sing all the same.

> "We're ten contented children
> From all across the land
> And if you like our merry song
> Do join our happy band
>
> We clean our shoes each morning
> And keep our bedrooms neat
> We never pick our noses
> And always wipe our feet
>
> We never fight or squabble
> Or call each other names
> But charm folk with our singing
> And play nice quiet games
>
> O children, when you meet us
> Pray do not scream and run
> But follow our example
> For goodness can be fun!"

Flora and Hilary were shocked. They could think of nothing to say.

"I must add that we are all especially fond of green vegetables," said the biggest girl.

"And we never wee in the bath," squeaked the smallest boy.

The Tractor Princess snorted. "Let's sort them out," she said, grabbing a girl by the ringlets.

"Don't hurt them," shouted Hilary. "Just get them dirty."

When the Best Behaved Children were nicely muddy, Hilary took a crumpled bag from his pocket.

"No hard feelings," he said. "Have a pineapple chunk."

The Best Behaved Children looked disgusted.

"Thank you, but I would prefer a dried banana," they all said at once.

"Have it your own way," said Hilary. With Flora hot on his heels, he ducked into the nearest marquee, where a man with very thick spectacles was peering at the labels on the sandwiches.

"Ermine and walnut ... swan and egg ... bison, lettuce and tomato ... wonderful reception," he said to Hilary. "But funnily enough, I haven't bumped into anyone I know. Haven't even spotted the Happy Couple yet."

"What happy couple?" asked Flora.

"Eleanor and that chap, whats-his-name — you know, the one she's just married."

"But this isn't a wedding reception," said Flora. "It's one of my mum's awful garden parties."

"Is that so?" said the man in amazement. "Daffodil, my dove, we're in the wrong tent. This is somebody's garden party."

ly?" said Daffodil. "I wonder who I ... ...e present to then?"

...ra helped herself to a sandwich. "How on earth did you get here?" she asked.

"I've no idea," said the man. "We just left the church and followed the hats, and here we are."

Hilary stared at him. "You don't look like a Mayor," he said. "Who are you?"

"Augustus and Daffodil Gravy-Browning, publishers, at your service," said the man with a little bow. "And who are you?"

"I expect you had a wonderful time helping to get everything ready" said Daffodil, when the children had introduced themselves. "I used to love playing in tents."

"No such luck!" grunted Flora.

"My Wicked Uncle has caused us great suffering," added Hilary gravely. They went on to tell the Gravy-Brownings how they had been imprisoned in the towers making pastry and ironing tablecloths (but they didn't tell them how naughty they had been, of course).

Just as the children were finishing their tale, a fanfare sounded. Everyone in the marquee threw down their cups and sandwiches and rushed outside.

"Whatever's going on?" asked Mr Gravy-Browning. "Is there a bomb scare?"

"Oh no, this always happens," said Flora. "Come and see!"

They followed her out of the tent and into the gardens, where, high up on a platform above an enormous crowd, Flora's parents sat on their thrones. One by one, their guests climbed the steps, then bowed or curtseyed to the Queen, who gave them her special wave and a balloon. Then they turned to the King, who handed them something and said, "This way out. Thank you."

"What's he got there?" asked Daffodil.

"Party-bags," explained Flora. "Otherwise they won't leave till midnight."

Beyond the garden walls they heard a great and growing commotion, as the guests swapped presents, blew whistles, sounded squeakers, and popped balloons. Everyone was very pleased and happy; everyone, that is, but the Best Behaved Children, who were so disgusted by a whoopee cushion that they didn't even notice their sweets.

There is almost as much work to be done after a garden party as there is beforehand. The following morning, the Nine Musical Brothers sang songs about washing up whilst the servants cleaned the crockery in the fountains.

"That was a waste of time," grumbled Flora, as she loaded the dirty tablecloths into her trailer.

"I'll say," agreed Hilary. "All that work, and not a thing to show for it."

"You poor, dear children," said a kind voice.

Flora and Hilary looked round and saw two rather odd-looking ladies. One was exceedingly bony, while the other was short and plump and very untidy.

"Dear Mr Gravy-Browning got in touch, so we came right away," said the plump one. "My name is Crump, Mavis Crump."

"And I am Miss Monica Crispbread," said the Bony Lady. "We'd like a word with you."

Nanny was dozing by the television that evening, when she awoke with a start.

"... And finally," the Newsreader was saying, "Her Royal Highness, the Tractor Princess, and her cousin, Prince Hilary of Etcetera-Etcetera, have just taken up their first charity posts."

Nanny beamed. "There's good in everyone," she said to herself.

The Newsreader went on, "Princess Flora is to be Patron of the National Society for the Abolition of Ironing. Members of the Society are recognized by their crumpled appearance and general lack of buttons ..."

Nanny dropped three stitches on the dish-cloth she was knitting.

"The Princess will be leading the Society's annual march and rally on November the third ... Prince Hilary, meanwhile, is to be President of the League for the Defence of Frozen Pastry. His first duty is to judge their annual cake-making competition."

"Cake-making   competition?"   echoed Nanny in disbelief.

"Viewers may be surprised to learn that in this competition, all home-made cakes are instantly disqualified. There are just two categories; the best results from a packet-mix, and the best ... "

Nanny ran to fetch Cook. When they came into the room, Monica Crispbread was saying to a reporter:

"And it doesn't stop at frozen pastry — we

aim to include packet stuffing and gravy-granules by the end of the year."

Cook unplugged the television. "Sub-versives," she said with a snort.

"There's no justice in this world," sighed Nanny. And so saying, she sewed a name-tape in her hairnet.

6

CHRISTMAS

Very early on Christmas morning, Flora slid down the banisters and into the ballroom. A long row of stockings hung over the fireplace, bulging and spilling with surprises. All except one, and that was the one with the little orange tractor on it. The princess snatched it, shook it, and stared in disbelief as a tiny tangerine and a chocolate walnut rolled across the floor.

It really hadn't been her fault about the Nativity play, she thought miserably: the Innkeeper had kicked her first. But smelly old Nanny must have told Father Christmas, and now she hadn't got any presents. She was about to throw the stocking at the window when she realised there was something left inside. Caught up in the wool was a little golden key; and attached to the key was a slip of paper. "Have left your present round the back. Too big for stocking. Regards, F.C."

Have left your present round the back - Too big for stocking. Regards F.C

Still in her pyjamas, Flora stepped outside and looked about her. There was no moon, but by the lights on the Christmas tree she could see an enormous parcel near one of the cannons. She tore along the terrace and ripped off the wrapping paper. Inside was a red and green shiny snowplough; it was rather small for a snowplough, but just the right size for a princess, and it had everything: flashing red lights and caterpillar tracks, a tank full of petrol and a useful toolbox. The only thing missing was snow.

Flora turned the key in the ignition, and drove slowly along the terrace, bumped down the steps and chugged up to the temple. She was practising a three point turn when the cathedral clock struck six. Nanny would still be asleep. Feeling very naughty, the princess steered back to the palace and out through the gates, past the tomb of the unknown soldier, round the block and up to the corner shop. It was open already, so she bought some bubble gum, then went back to the palace for a bacon sandwich.

After breakfast, and unwrapping the presents, the Royal Family went to the carol service in the cathedral. When they got back they had to park their carriages in the road, for the forecourt was filled with television vans. The Queen felt weak at the knees when she saw them. Whatever had possessed her to agree to a live broadcast, today of all days! She hurried indoors to finish writing her speech.

Flora felt quite differently. She leapt from her carriage to help unload the lights, then helped carry the television cameras to the Throne Room. She was eating her third hot dog from the mobile canteen when she noticed that the door of the Outside Broadcast van was open. She peeped inside. There was

nobody there, so she sat on a swivelly chair and twiddled some buttons. She was just about to pull a lever that said "Aerial" when a furious voice shouted: "Get out of my van at once!"

Flora took one look at the man in the anorak and fled. She had never seen anyone so angry.

Down in the kitchens, the Nine Musical Brothers were busily beating and chopping and peeling and stirring and sifting and mixing and slicing and sifting and grating around the great wooden table. Cook had gone to visit her sister, and the Brothers had begged to be allowed to cook the Christmas dinner.

"Yuletide Greetings," beamed Nanny. She had holly on her bonnet, and a sprig of mistletoe on her spectacle chain.

"Have any of you boys seen Mr Chaucer? I know he's coming for dinner."

They all shook their heads.

"Saw him in church," said one.

"Have you looked in the garage?" asked another.

"An excellent suggestion," said Nanny.

As soon as she was gone, Chaucer crawled

out from under the table with a sigh of relief. He helped himself to a mince pie and hurried up to the Dark Red Drawing Room, where the Queen introduced him to three kings who were staying in the State Apartments. They were very impressed with the Christmas decorations, especially the ones in the gallery. The King had been up until midnight, putting glitter on the pictures and paper hats on all the statues.

When all the wine had gone, and everyone was looking hungrily at the last mince pie, the dinner gong sounded.

The Nine Musical Brothers had prepared a feast fit for a king and full of surprises; there were feathers in the gravy and a beak in the bread sauce and the sprouts had been salted nine times. Midway through the meal there

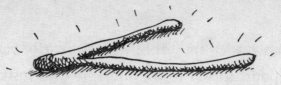

was a hurrumph! from Nanny. She plucked the wishbone from her gravy and held it up triumphantly.

"Let me pull it! Let me pull it!" squealed Flora. She had a very important wish to make.

Nanny and Flora tugged until the bone snapped exactly in half.

"I've got it!" they both shouted at once.

"You both get a wish," said the Queen firmly.

After the pies and the pudding and the crystallised fruit, the Queen slipped upstairs to pin on her medals. It would soon be time for her speech. Flora crept away too, in case she was told to wash up. She went straight to the Throne Room to watch the television crew at work. What a lot of people there were; and what a lot they had brought with them! You couldn't see the ceiling for spotlights, and the floor was simply wriggling with wires and cables. The gold furniture was piled up at one end of the room and both thrones had disappeared beneath piles of coats. The Queen's desk stood alone in a corner, trapped by cameras and complicated equipment.

Then something interesting happened.

People began to shout and argue and hit one another with clipboards. Three ladies in headphones hid under the sofa, and the man in the anorak kicked himself. Nobody noticed Flora.

"OI!" she yelled. "What's going on?"

"We seem to have misplaced our microphone, Your Highness," said the man in the anorak.

"You forgot to bring it, you mean," shrilled a voice from under the sofa.

"Why can't you go and fetch it? There must be thirty cars outside," said Flora.

"There's three feet of snow as well," said Anorak gloomily. "Or hadn't you noticed?"

Flora couldn't believe her luck. Her wish had come true! A man drew her a map on the back of a Christmas card, while the producer disappeared to make a telephone call. When he came back he said: "It's all arranged, Your Highness. But you'd better leave at once — there's less than an hour to go."

In the courtyard, Flora siphoned the petrol from somebody's car, just in case. Then she pulled on her goggles and a balaclava helmet, climbed into her snowplough and set off with the television crew waving and cheering from

the balcony. There was nothing they could do but sit and wait.

The little Princess drove through the narrow streets, thick with snow and the smell of dinner. Past the cathedral and dark shut shops, round silent squares with frozen fountains, on and on, until she reached Television Buildings. A caretaker stood at the gate, wearing a party hat and slippers. He handed Flora a silver case. "Weathermen were wrong again," he said mournfully.

There were just minutes to go when Flora burst into the Throne Room clutching the silver case. It was seized by the sound engineers, who set to work at once with the wiring.

"Three cheers for the Tractor Princess," called the props man.

"Hip, hip"

"HOORAY!"

"Hip, hip"

"HOORAY!"

"Hip, hip"

"HOORAY!"

Then Anorak said "Your Highness, you must name your reward: it shall be yours, no matter what the cost."

"I'd like to help in the control van when you broadcast Mummy's speech."

Anorak turned pale. He could forget all about that knighthood now.

It was the best speech the Queen had ever given. She didn't cough, or twitch or hesitate once; but nobody noticed, for outside in the control room, her daughter was trying some special effects.

All over the Kingdom people got up to adjust their televisions as the Queen began to

fade: when she reappeared, she whirled madly about like a towel in a tumble drier. Eventually she came to rest upside down, and stayed that way while she spoke of her Australian tour, growing redder and redder as Flora fiddled with the filters. Then suddenly she righted herself, and five little Queens appeared on the screen, all talking at once. Flora giggled and twiddled even more knobs. Now the Queen looked perfectly normal: but her voice seemed strange. She sounded as though she were speaking from the bottom of a well, and then from the depths of a cardboard box. At the end of her speech, she wished all her subjects a Merry Christmas (in a robot voice) and a Happy New Year (in an underwater voice). Then the Nine Musical Brothers sang the National Anthem, and it was all over for another year.

The Queen was surprised how quickly everyone packed up and left: they threw everything into bags and boxes and fled along the corridors to the courtyard. The convoy of cars and vans, the Celebrity Coach, the mobile canteen and the Outside Broadcast unit all crept along the track cleared by the Tractor Princess. Only the cross man in the anorak was left; his car wouldn't start, because Flora had siphoned off his petrol. He ran and skidded all the way back to Television Buildings and locked himself in the basement.

When the television crew had gone, there was tea and Christmas cake in the Throne Room. Nanny organised all kinds of games, Statues and Charades and Musical Bumps,

Postman's Knock and Blind Man's Buff. Then the King suggested everyone should perform a party piece.

It was Nanny's turn first. Then Chaucer juggled some Christmas puddings. Afterwards, he went to sit down beside Nanny.

"I did enjoy your impression of a chicken," he said with a wink. "Would you do it again, just for me?"

Nanny blushed and twittered.

"Oh, I couldn't," she said.

"Oh, go on," begged Chaucer.

So she did, and he kissed her under the mistletoe.

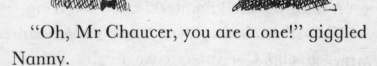

"Oh, Mr Chaucer, you are a one!" giggled Nanny.

Then the Nine Musical Brothers sang "Rudolf the Red-Nosed Reindeer" very nicely in Latin: the King told some elephant jokes, and the Queen wiggled her ears.

The Tractor Princess astonished everyone. She didn't swing from the chandelier or somersault over the sofa or even play the spoons.

She just twirled about the Christmas tree in a pretty dress.

"A proper princess at last," sobbed the Queen.

"A dainty little daughter!" cried the King.

Flora curtsied nicely to her parents and turned to Chaucer.

"Didn't think I'd do it, did you?" she said triumphantly.

Chaucer looked a little peeved. "You win all right; but it's the last time I'm having a bet with you," he said, throwing her a bunch of keys. "Third garage on the right — and don't forget to wear your goggles."

Nanny was barring Flora's way.

"You're not going out in that monstrous thing now, my girl," she said crossly.

"I know," smiled Flora sweetly. "I'm going to respray Daddy's limousine."

ROSIE RUMPOLE
written and illustrated by
Annemie Heymans

Rosie sometimes gets tired of being the littlest in the family, especially with three older brothers. But her toys are her real friends and they have lots of adventures together.

Here are eight short stories about Rosie, her toys and the friendly neighbours.

EMILY AND MR PRENDERGAST
by Shirley Isherwood
Illustrations by Dorothy Tucker

There once was a little girl called Emily who had a cat who could speak. His name was Mr Prendergast.

It was wonderful to have Mr Prendergast as a friend, and Emily loved him dearly, but he did seem to get her into a great deal of trouble for carrying out his eccentric ideas.

Here are twelve stories about the adventures of Emily and her unusual cat.